This edition published by Parragon in 2012
Parragon
Chartist House
15-17 Trim Street
Bath BA1 1HA, UK
www.parragon.com

Edited by Samantha Crockford
Designed by Pete Hampshire
Production by Emma Fulleylove

ISBN 978-1-4454-7392-5

Printed in China

# DISNEY · PIXAR
# Cars

# STORYBOOK COLLECTION

Bath · New York · Singapore · Hong Kong · Cologne · Delhi
Melbourne · Amsterdam · Johannesburg · Shenzhen

# THIS BOOK BELONGS TO

......................................................

# CONTENTS

# THE STORY
# OF THE FILM

Lightning McQueen was taking part in the biggest race of the season – the Dinoco 400. Also racing was Lightning's rival, Chick Hicks, and the current champion, The King. This would be The King's last ever race, which meant the lucrative Dinoco sponsorship was up for grabs.

When Lightning pulled into the pits, he filled up with petrol but ignored his crew's advice to change tyres. He increased his lead, but it was risky.

In the last lap his back tyres blew. Chick and The King drew level with him just as he limped across the finishing-line.

It was too close to call!

While Lightning waited for the race results, he posed for the reporters, pushing his pit crew aside. Furious, they quit on the spot. Then the announcement came. "Ladies and gentlemen, for the first time in Piston Cup history we have a three-way tie!"

A tie-breaker race would be held in California in one week.

Lightning ordered his truck, Mack, to drive through the night to California. He promised Mack that he would stay up with him, but he soon fell asleep.

Many hours later, a gang of cars pulled alongside the exhausted truck and began bumping him for a laugh. Mack swerved dangerously and Lightning was thrown out of the trailer on to the road.

Lightning woke up to oncoming traffic! He thought he saw Mack pull off the road and quickly followed, but it wasn't Mack and he was lost.

Feeling panicked, Lightning tore off up the main street of a small town, destroying everything in his path. He ended up dangling helplessly between two telegraph poles!

"Boy, you're in a heap of trouble," said the Sheriff.

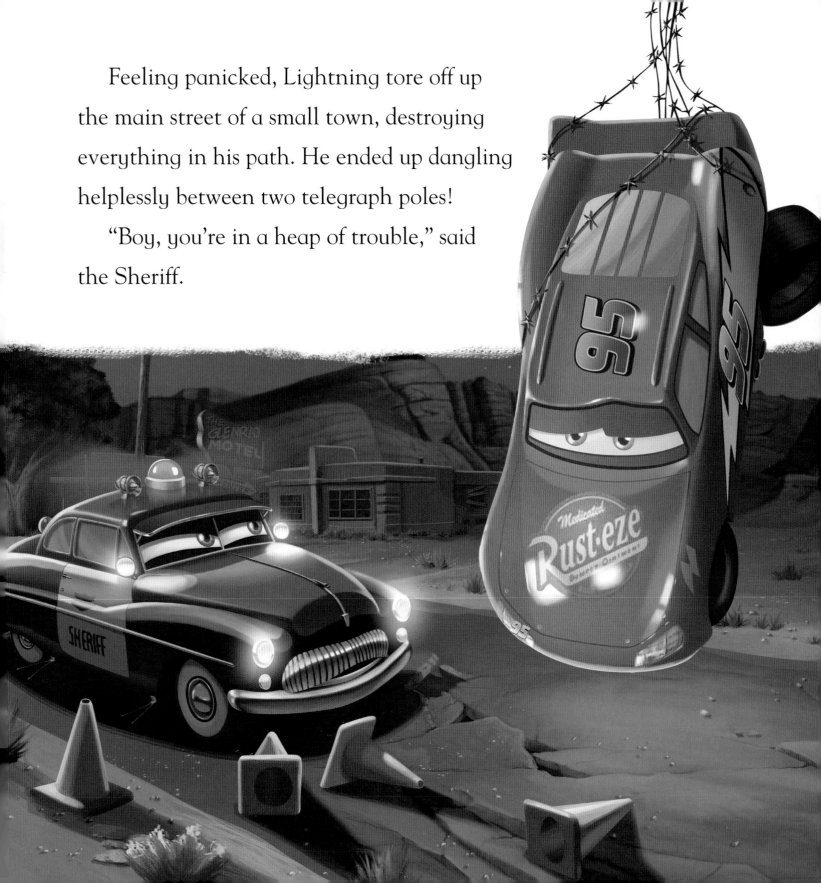

The next morning Lightning woke up to see a cheery tow truck grinning at him from the gates of an impound lot.

"Hi, there! My name's Mater," he said. "Welcome to Radiator Springs!"

At that moment, the Sheriff arrived to escort Lightning to court. The judge, Doc Hudson, wanted to kick Lightning out of town, but Sally, the attorney, had a better idea; Lightning couldn't leave until he had repaired the town's damaged road.

Reluctantly, Lightning set to work pulling Bessie, the enormous road-surfacing machine. When he heard a radio report that Chick was already in California practising for the tie-breaker race, he pulled Bessie as hard and fast as he could.

A couple of hours later, Lightning announced that the road was finished. But it was a total mess. "Now it matches the rest of the town," sneered Lightning.

Doc was furious. He decided to settle matters with a race.

"If you win, you go and I fix the road. If I win, you do the road my way," he said.

Out at the dirt track, Lightning took a quick lead. But he misjudged a tricky bend and wiped out!

Mater hauled the humiliated Lightning out of the ditch and he was sent back to work. By the next morning Radiator Springs had a patch of beautifully surfaced road.

Lightning was tired and filthy, but the townsfolk thanked him.

That night, Mater took Lightning tractor tipping. Mater sneaked up on a sleeping tractor and honked. The startled tractor woke up and fell over! When it was Lightning's turn, he revved his engine so loudly, all the tractors keeled over at one time. Mater and Lightning could not stop laughing.

As they returned to the motel, Mater showed off his amazing backwards-driving tricks. Lightning was impressed.

"Maybe I'll use it in my big race," Lightning said thoughtfully.

When Lightning told Mater that winning the race meant getting a new sponsor with private helicopters, Mater got excited. He asked if he could ride in a helicopter some day! Lightning agreed casually.

Sally had overheard Lightning and Mater's conversation. "Did you mean it?" she asked. "You know, Mater trusts you."

The next morning, Lightning saw three Piston Cups in Doc's shop!
He was amazed. Doc Hudson was a racing legend!

Doc was furious when he found Lightning in his shop.

"All I see is a bunch of empty cups," Doc said, pushing Lightning out
and slamming the door.

Lightning rushed over to Flo's Café to tell everyone that Doc was a famous race car. But no one believed him. While the other cars were laughing, Sally filled Lightning's tank. Sheriff worried that Lightning would escape, but Sally surprised everyone – including Lightning.

"I trust him," she said.

"Let's go for a drive," Sally suggested. The two cars zoomed up a mountain road and Lightning realized he was racing just for fun for the first time. He also noticed how beautiful the scenery – and Sally – were.

24

Sally told Lightning how she had been an attorney in L.A. but hadn't been happy. She just drove and drove until she reached Radiator Springs.

"I fell in love – with this," Sally continued. Far below lay a gorgeous valley surrounded by copper-coloured mountains. In the distance, Lightning saw cars speeding past on the Interstate.

"They don't even know what they're missing," he murmured.

Later that day, Lightning saw Doc roaring around the dirt racetrack.

"You're amazing!" Lightning told the old pro. But Doc raced off.

Lightning followed Doc to his office.

"How could you quit at the top of your game?" Lightning asked.

Doc showed Lightning a newspaper article about a wreck he had been in. After he was repaired, Doc wanted to return to racing. But he had been replaced – by a rookie.

The next morning, the road was finished. But where was Lightning? Had he left for California? Everyone felt sad.

But just then, Lightning rolled up. He hadn't left!

"I knew you wouldn't go without saying goodbye!" Mater exclaimed.

Lightning explained that he had a few things to do before leaving. He spent the rest of the day using every shop in town. He got new tyres, a new paint job and fuel from Fillmore – Lightning liked helping the town's small businesses....

...and Lightning liked teaming up with his new friends!

"Is it getting dark out?" he called loudly when Sally drove up. Suddenly Radiator Springs lit up in glowing neon colours and music played. It was time to cruise!

But as the townsfolk drove in pairs together, a helicopter searchlight swept over them.

"We have found Lightning McQueen!" boomed a voice from a loudspeaker.

News vans swarmed into town. Reporters surrounded Lightning, shouting questions. He couldn't see Sally or reach his friends.

Lightning's agent wanted Lightning to leave Radiator Springs straight away. Lightning and Sally gazed at each other. Neither of them knew what to say.

"Good luck in California." Sally said at last.

"I hope you find what you're looking for."

Once Lightning had gone, Sally discovered it was Doc who gave away Lightning's location. "It's best for everyone, Sally," Doc explained.

Sally was shocked. "Or best for you?"

In a packed stadium in California, the tiebreaker race for the Piston Cup started. But Lightning couldn't concentrate. He kept remembering his friends in Radiator Springs. Somehow, winning no longer seemed that important to Lightning.

Just then Doc's voice came over the radio: "I didn't come all this way to see you quit."

Lightning saw his Radiator Springs friends in his pit – with Doc as his crew chief! "If you can drive as good as you can fix a road, then you can win this race with your eyes shut," Doc said.

Inspired by his friends, Lightning tore around the track, closing the gap. Chick tried his usual dirty tricks, but Lightning remembered what his friends had taught him.

Lightning was in the lead! Chick and The King were fighting for second place. But then, Chick rammed the veteran race car. The King hit a wall and flipped.

When Lightning saw The King's crumpled body, he remembered Doc's final crash. Lightning screeched to a stop – inches from the finish line.

As Chick won the race, Lightning drove over to The King. He thought the veteran should finish his last race. As he pushed The King over the finish line, the crowd erupted in cheers.

Chick won the Piston Cup, but Lightning was the hero of the race!

Tex, Dinoco's owner, asked Lightning, "How would you like to be the new face of Dinoco?"

Lightning politely refused, deciding to stay loyal to his original sponsor.

A little later, back in Radiator Springs, Lightning found Sally. They heard someone wildly yelling, "Wooo-hoo!" It was Mater, taking his first helicopter ride! Sally smiled. Lightning had remembered his promise.

She smiled before speeding off down the mountain, with Lightning close behind. It looked as if the rookie race car had found his new home.

## The End

# GUIDO'S BIG SURPRISE

Luigi was bursting with excitement. He was planning a racing-themed surprise party for his assistant and best friend, Guido. They were both big racing fans.

Guido rolled to a stop beside his friend outside Casa Della Tires.

"Today is-a going to be a good-a day, eh, Guido?" Luigi said.

The little forklift sighed. Then he turned and went into the store, ready to get to work.

Luigi chuckled. "He has-a no idea! My friend is-a in for a big-a surprise."

Just then, Ramone pulled up. "Hey, man, I'm here for my new tyres," he said.

"Perfecto!" Luigi exclaimed. "Come on-a inside."

"Has Guido figured out the surprise?" Ramone whispered before they went in.

"No, it's-a still a secret," Luigi replied.

Luigi and Ramone went inside. "Guido," Luigi said, "Signore Ramone is here for his-a new tyres."

Guido went into the back room to get them.

"How is your-a lovely lady, Flo?" Luigi asked Ramone.

"She's doing fine," Ramone said as Guido reappeared. "She just got a new shipment of fuel that is mighty smooth. You should stop in for a sip."

"Yes, maybe we'll-a come over later." Luigi winked at Ramone. He knew that the surprise party would take place at Flo's V8 Café. Then he noticed the tyres Guido had found. Two were flat and the other two were covered with mud.

"Guido," Luigi said slowly, "I put those-a tyres in the junk pile this-a morning."

The little forklift looked at the tyres he was holding and his eyes widened. He hurried back to the storeroom.

"He looks blue, man," Ramone said.

Luigi frowned. "Of course he looks-a blue. He is always the colour blue."

Ramone laughed. "No, I meant that Guido looks sad."

When Guido returned with the correct tyres, Luigi watched him. Guido did look sad. Luigi hoped the party would cheer him up.

"What's-a bugging you, Guido?" Luigi asked later.

But the only response was a loud, "Ka-chow!" as Lightning McQueen rolled into the store, followed by Mater.

"Hey, guys," said Lightning, "I'm here to practise for my next big race. You'll be my pit crew again. Right, Guido?"

The forklift nodded.

"Here's the plan," Lightning said. "Picture me speeding down the track. You be ready for the pit stop, okay?"

"He's-a ready," Luigi answered.

Guido got into his pit-stop position.

*Vroom.* "I'm heading for the pit stop," Lightning pretended, "and you're ready to change my tyres in 2.5 seconds flat. And... go!"

Guido set to work. Luigi and Mater counted. But Guido was working very slowly.

"Two and a half-a," Luigi said, drawing out the numbers. "Three-a..."

"Three, four, five," Mater counted.

It took Guido five seconds – double his usual time!

"Mamma mia!" Luigi exclaimed. "Uh... Guido didn't sleep-a so good last night. Tomorrow, he will be back to his-a speedy self."

Lightning nodded, but he looked worried. He turned and followed Mater out of the store.

"Hey, buddy, what would our country be called if every car was painted pink?" the tow truck said. He barely paused before shouting, "A pink carnation! Get it? 'Car' and 'nation'."

Luigi turned to his friend. "What's-a wrong, Guido?" he asked. "You cannot go on being down in the Dumpster."

"Hello, boys," Sally said as she rolled in. "There's a customer at my motel who needs her tyres checked. Do you have some time?"

Guido perked up a little. He went to grab his toolbox.

"Guido will take-a good care of her," Luigi said.

Sally smiled. "I knew I could count on you guys. Come on, Guido. I'll take you over to meet her." Then she turned back to Luigi and said, "I'm heading over to Flo's afterwards if you need me."

"Grazie, Sally," Luigi replied.

After Guido left, Luigi circled the shop, cleaning things up. He saw a wrench lying on the floor and went to put it with the rest of Guido's tools. When Luigi opened the chest, he saw a postcard from Italy. It was from Guido's cousin, Guidoni.

Luigi gasped. "Guido is-a homesick! That's-a why he's so sad."

Luigi put the wrench and the card in the chest. Then he raced over to Flo's. They had to change their racing-themed surprise party to a grand Italian celebration.

Flo was serving drinks to Lightning, Sally, Mater and Ramone at her café when Luigi appeared.

"He's-a sick!" Luigi exclaimed.

The other cars gathered around him.

"Who's sick?" Sally asked.

"Guido!" Luigi cried. "He's-a homesick for his family in Italy. I thought he was-a missing the excitement of a race. But now I'm sure he's been sad because he misses his-a home."

"Well," said Sally, "Guido has a home right here in Radiator Springs – and we're going to cheer him up."

"That's right," said Flo. "We'll just change our racing party to an Italian party! I'll see if Fillmore has an olive-oil-flavoured brew. That would be perfecto."

Lightning smiled. "You can count on me to bring Italian racing flags for decorations."

"And Flo's got some old Italian classics on the car-aoke machine," Ramone chimed in. "'Lugnut Prima' is one of our favourites."

Luigi smiled as his friends piped up with more ideas for the party. "Grazie," Luigi said. "This will mean-a so much to Guido."

Luigi left Flo, Sally and Ramone at the café to keep planning, while he went with Lightning and Mater to find Red the fire truck. They had a great idea for a big finale.

Luckily, Red agreed. He couldn't wait to be part of the surprise.

That night, Luigi could barely contain his excitement. "It's-a been a long day, eh, Guido," he said. "What do you say we go over to Flo's for a sip of oil?"

Guido gave a little nod, then followed Luigi out the door. When they arrived at Flo's, all of the inside lights were off. It looked like the café was closed. "I wonder what's-a going on?" Luigi said, trying to hide a smile. "Let's go in and see."

As soon as they rolled into the café, the lights came on. "Viva Italiano, Guido!" Flo said. The other cars all cheered.

Guido looked around in awe. There were Italian flags hanging on the walls, and lots of red, white and green balloons filled the café.

There were posters of famous Italian landmarks. Mater stopped beside the one of the Leaning Tower of Tyres. "Hey, this here picture looks a lot like the tower outside Luigi's store," he said.

Mater rolled up to the front of the café. "Can I have everyone's attention, please?"

Ramone dimmed the lights until a single spotlight shone on the tow truck.

"Now for a real surprise," he said. "Red will perform an Italian opera selection."

Red shyly moved into the spotlight. Flo started up the car-aoke machine. Beautiful music filled the air and Red began to sing.

"Mamma mia!" Luigi said. "It's bellissimo."

Guido closed his eyes as he listened. He felt like he was back home in Italy listening to opera with his family.

When Red finished, all the cars were speechless. The fire truck quickly moved out of the spotlight.

"Red, that was just beautiful," Sally said.

"You made this-a night so very special," Luigi said.

Red smiled shyly.

Flo set to work making sure everyone had enough oil. Mater told Red and Lightning some more jokes.

Luigi pulled his friend aside. "You are-a happy again now?" he asked Guido.

The little forklift beamed and waved an Italian flag. There was no need to be homesick when he was already right at home in Radiator Springs.

## *The End*

# All's Well at the
# Wheel Well

Radiator Springs was bustling with activity. The grand reopening of the Wheel Well Motel was in less than a week.

Sally the shiny blue sports car was very excited. Ever since the famous race car Lightning McQueen had moved his racing headquarters to Radiator Springs, the town had been filled with visitors. When all the rooms at the Cozy Cone Motel had been booked for weeks and weeks, Sally decided it was time to reopen the Wheel Well.

"Radiator Springs is back on the map," she had told her friends. "Now, we need another motel for all the cars that visit."

The townsfolk had agreed with Sally. They were happy to see visitors return to the town. And they were eager to help Sally fix up the old motel.

"We'll be the most popular place in Carburetor County!" Sally cheered.

Ramone helped Sally decorate the rooms inside the motel. He gave each one its own style. "Then cars will want to return to check out the different looks," the hot rod explained.

Sally's favourite was a room overlooking the valley. Ramone had painted a mural of Radiator Springs at night showing the stores with their neon lights.

"This is great, Ramone!" Sally exclaimed. "My two favourite views are in one room."

While Ramone fixed up the inside of the motel, Red helped Sally spruce up the outside.

The fire engine had created new flower displays for the motel. He watered each patch once a day and drove out to the motel at least twice more to make sure everything looked perfect for the grand reopening.

When Lightning McQueen rolled back into town, he found Mater, Flo and Sheriff at Flo's V8 Café.

"Welcome back, buddy," the tow truck said with a wide smile. "We sure missed you around here."

"Thanks, Mater. I'm glad to be home," Lightning said. The race car had been travelling to different events in the past few weeks. But no matter how many trophies he won, he was always eager to get back to Radiator Springs. "I love racing, but it's nice to slow down every now and then."

"Well, you don't have much time before things speed up here," Flo told him. "Sally's opening the new Wheel Well in just three days."

"Really? Is she ready? Maybe I should go out there and see if she needs any help," Lightning said.

"I'll race you!" Mater exclaimed. "Last one there has to clean my wheel wells!"

A few minutes later, Lightning skidded to a stop in front of the Wheel Well. He was just ahead of Mater.

"Aw, shucks," Mater said. "I almost had you."

"Next time I'll race you driving backwards. You'll win for sure," Lightning replied. He looked up at the motel. "Wow, Sally really has fixed this place up."

"Everybody helped," Mater said. "I got to tow old shrubs out of the way so Red could plant the new flowers. And I promised Miss Sally I would give all her customers free backwards driving lessons!"

The two cars rolled over to Guido and Luigi. They'd brought some tyres out from Luigi's store, Casa Della Tires. Guido was creating a new tyre display for the reopening.

"You are just in-a time," Luigi said, when he saw the race car and tow truck. "Guido is almost-a finished."

Guido put the last tyre into place. Then he rolled back to admire his work.

"It's a wheel… made of wheels," Lightning said slowly.

"That's-a right!" Luigi crowed proudly.

"Hey, Stickers," Sally said as she drove over. "When did you get back to town?"

"Just a little while ago," Lightning replied. "This place looks great, Sally. Is there anything I can do to help you get ready?"

"You've already done more than enough," Sally said. "You brought customers back to our town by setting up your racing headquarters here." She smiled and went to check on one of the rooms.

"Miss Sally sure does like you," Mater said to his friend. *"Whoo-eee!"*

"Oh, come on, Mater. Sally's just excited about reopening the motel. I wish I could think of something to do to make the day even more special for her," Lightning said. "I'm gonna go for a drive. Maybe that will help me think."

"Okay, buddy," Mater said. "Just remember to keep your wheels on the road!"

Lightning drove down the mountain and through the valley. He passed the old dirt track he used to practise on. He slowed down as he rolled into the centre of town.

The cars that weren't helping out at the Wheel Well were getting their stores ready for the extra customers who would come for the reopening. Lightning saw Lizzie out in front of her store, Radiator Springs Curios. He rolled over to say hello.

"Stanley would have gotten all steamed up if he could see the town today," Lizzie said. "Why, the Wheel Well was one of his favourite spots!"

Lizzie slapped a sticker on Lightning's front bumper and went back to tidying up her shop.

Lightning looked at the bumper sticker in a reflection on an old hubcap. It read: ALL'S WELL AT THE WHEEL WELL. He smiled. Lizzie always had the perfect sticker.

Lightning left Lizzie, but he couldn't stop thinking of what she'd said about Stanley, who had founded the town. If only he could see Radiator Springs today!

Then he thought about what Sally had said – that he'd been the one to bring visitors back to town.

"All because of a little racing," he murmured. Suddenly, he had an idea!

A race car couldn't paint rooms at the motel or sell stickers. But he could help Sally make headlines at the opening with a trick or two. He zoomed off to tell Sally his idea – and to start practising.

For the next two days, Lightning worked on his trick.
Mater drove out to the old track and watched him take turn
after turn. "You're up to something!" he called out to his friend.
Lightning only smiled and kept practising.

The morning of the grand reopening, the cars from Radiator Springs were gathered in front of the Wheel Well with press cars and visitors. Everyone was excited. The cars oohed and aahed over the motel.

"Ladies and gentlecars," Sally greeted everyone. "It is my pleasure to welcome you to the historic Wheel Well Motel, once again open to all the travellers who come to Radiator Springs. And now, to kick off the festivities, Lightning McQueen would like to give you an official Wheel Well welcome!"

There was a loud *vroom*. Lightning zipped around the press cars. When he was right in front of Sally, he turned and lifted his two left wheels at the same time to wave to the crowd.

The press cars snapped photos, and the crowd cheered loudly.

Then Lightning looped around Sally and waved with his two right wheels.

The crowd went wild.

A few minutes later, Sally invited everyone inside for a tour. She stood by the door and welcomed each car.

When Lightning pulled up beside her, she smiled. "You really got the crowd excited about the motel. You care about this town a lot."

Lightning beamed. "Getting lost here was the best thing that ever happened to me," he said. "It's my home."

Sally looked at the bumper sticker on Lightning's front fender. "Nice sticker," she said as she rolled inside.

Lightning laughed as he followed her. All *was* well at the Wheel Well... and in Radiator Springs.

## The End

# THE BIG SHOW

Life in Radiator Springs was nice and easy for Lightning McQueen. He drove slowly down Main Street, taking in the sights and sounds of the town.

The race car smiled wide as he pulled into Tow Mater Towing and Salvage. His friend Mater grinned and drove over beside him.

"Hey there, buddy," the tow truck said. "Aren't you a sight for sore eyes!"

"I'm in the mood for a little fun today, Mater," Lightning said. What do you say we come up with something amazing to do?"

Mater thought for a moment. "Want to go tractor tipping?" he asked.

"Nah. We did that last week," Lightning said.

"I know!" Mater grinned. "I can race you backwards to the firehouse!"

Lightning sighed. "That wouldn't be bad, but... I was hoping for something, well, bigger."

"Bigger," Mater repeated, nodding. "Bigger... bigger... "

They soon met some of the other cars over by the tyre shop. As they were talking Sally drove past, gleaming in the sunshine. She beeped hello.

"Hi, Sally! Bye, Sally!" Mater yelled.

Lightning flashed his lucky lightning-bolt sticker at her. "*Ka-ch* – Hey, what's her hurry? Oh, I know. I bet she's off to solve another legal crisis." Not only was Sally the prettiest car Lightning had ever seen, she was one of the smartest.

"Aw, did you see the way she shined her mirrors at you? That was just plum showing off," Mater said. "But, shoot, I'd be a show-off too if I was all pretty and clean like she is."

"You think she was showing off? For me?" Lightning asked.

"'Course I do," Mater replied. "A car like Sally was made for the spotlight."

Lightning smiled. "Mater! That's it. You're a genius!"

"I am?" The tow truck blinked.

"We'll round up everyone and have a good old-fashioned car show tonight!" Lightning exclaimed.

Mater grinned. "You always have the best ideas, buddy."

"Not without some inspiration from my best friend!" Lightning and Mater drove over to Flo's V8 Café for a breakfast fill-up.

The tow truck looked around. "Maybe Flo would let us have the show here?"

"Let's ask her!" Lightning said.

When Flo heard their idea, she lit up with excitement. "Oh, boy! That's the best idea I've heard in a long time!"

Flo had been a Motorama girl years ago before she came to Radiator Springs. She promised to give tips to any cars that wanted them. "After all, my days on the circuit taught me a lot about this kind of thing."

Lightning and Mater thanked Flo and hurried off to spread the word.

"This news is-a so good-a it makes me the happiest car in the world!" Luigi exclaimed. "It will mean big-a business for Casa Della Tires!"

Guido nodded excitedly.

Ramone was happy, too. "My appointment book's already filling up," he said as Mater and Lightning passed by Ramone's House of Body Art. "Good thing I just got a shipment of new paint colours."

"*Whee-hoo!* Folks sure do move fast," Mater said as they watched two cars dash into Fillmore's for some organic fuel and tie-dyed mud flaps.

"That's what I'm always telling you, Mater," Lightning said. "When it comes to having fun, it's all about... speed!"

The race car sped off towards the Wheel Well to find Sally. He couldn't wait to tell her about the show! He knew she would be thrilled.

"That sounds wonderful," Sally said when Lightning told her about the show. She was busy scheduling day trips for the customers at the Wheel Well. Since the motel had reopened, she spent all her free time making sure that visitors were happy.

"Everyone's really excited," Lightning said.

Sally smiled. "What a great way to boost everyone's spirits!"

They drove back into town. The businesses on Main Street were bustling with customers. Sarge waved as they drove past his army surplus store. "Make sure to get in line early for a car wash!" he called. "I waited for over an hour!"

"Luigi, would you have time to give me two new tyres?" Sally asked as she pulled up to the tyre shop. "Mine are getting a little worn down."

"For you, Miss Sally, anything!" Luigi exclaimed, waving her in. Lightning said goodbye and sped over to Ramone's. He was going to get some new lightning bolts!

After Sally got her new tyres, she headed for the car wash. She noticed a little grey car pulled over to the side of the street with his flashers on. He looked lost.

"Hi there. My name's Sally," she said, pulling up alongside him. "Do you need some help?"

"I'm Marty," the car said. "Where am I?"

"You're in Radiator Springs," Sally said proudly. "And you've arrived just in time for our first annual car show. It's tonight!"

The car looked nervous. "I'm afraid I can't stay around for a car show. I just got off the Interstate to get some gasoline."

"Come with me," Sally said, leading the way. "Flo's V8 Café has just what you need."

"Hey, Sally! Who's your new friend?" Mater called as they drove past. He and Fillmore were on the way to get their tyres rotated.

"Marty. He's just passing through," Sally explained.

As Marty's tank was filling up at Flo's, Sally studied a map. "You need to drive through Ornament Valley and continue on for about twenty miles," she said.

"Twenty miles?" Marty looked stressed. "I'm already late for a meeting!"

"There is a shortcut," Sally said. "But it will take you through some bumpy territory." She wasn't sure the frazzled car was up to the challenge.

Marty took a big gulp of gasoline. "Do you think you'd be able to show me?"

"Well..." Sally broke off as Lightning zoomed up.

"Check this out!" He showed off his new lightning bolts. "Cars from far and wide have heard about our show. Cool, huh?"

Sally laughed. "Really cool." She introduced Marty to Lightning. "He is in a hurry and I'm trying to help him."

"Sally's the best map reader in town," Lightning said. "She'll help you get wherever you need to go."

"So, can you show me the way?" Marty asked again.

"But what about the car show?" Lightning cried.

"If we leave now I'll be back in plenty of time," Sally declared.

"Let me take him," Lightning offered. "I don't want you to miss the show."

But Sally knew Lightning would be too fast for Marty to follow.

"I know these roads better than anyone," Sally said. "I'll be back before you know it!"

Lightning waved goodbye as Sally and Marty set off. "Come back and visit!" he said.

Sally and Marty drove to Ornament Valley. When they reached the shortcut, Sally slowed down. The road wasn't well-marked. If Marty made a wrong turn, he'd be even more lost.

She took a deep breath. "This way," she said, turning onto the dusty old mountain road.

When they reached the Interstate, Marty gave Sally a grateful beep goodbye. Sally sped back towards Radiator Springs.

She made it in time for the car show... but she was covered with dust and one of her tyres was quickly losing air!

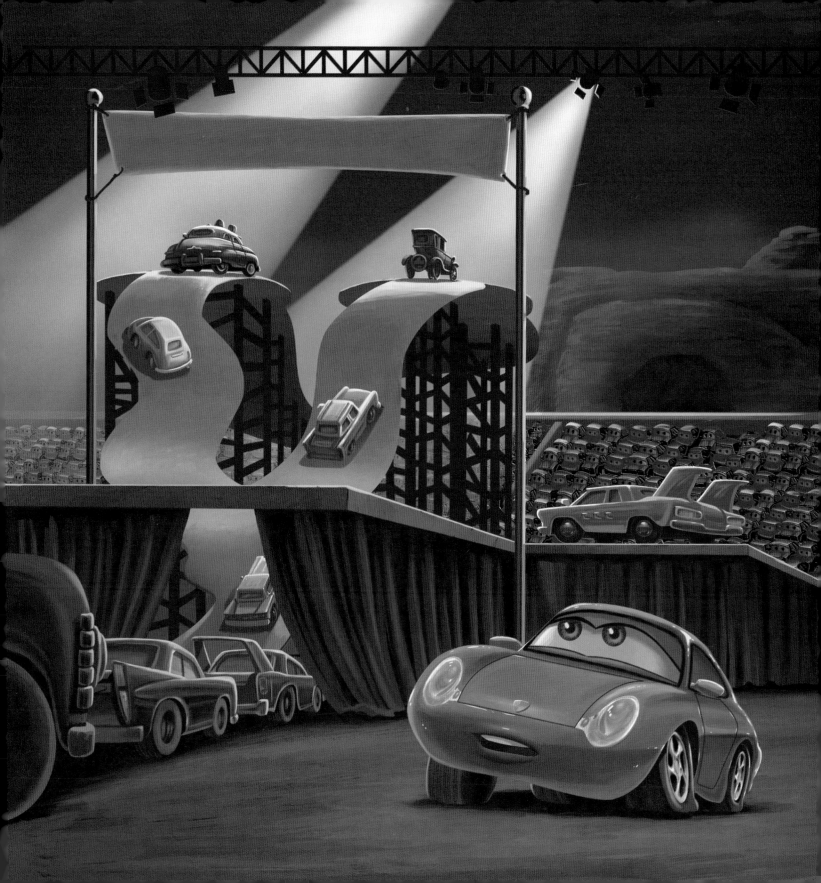

Flo spotted Sally. "You're just in time!" she exclaimed.

"I think it's too late," Sally replied as she watched all the shiny cars drive past.

"It's never too late!" Lightning zoomed up with Red and Luigi. In minutes, the fire engine had hosed off the dust and Luigi had fitted her with a new tyre.

"You guys are the best!" Sally declared. She drove up to the stage for her turn in the spotlight.

"Sally, you're the prettiest car here!" Mater shouted.

The sports car beamed. "Thanks, Mater," she said. She'd never felt like such a star.

## The End

# SNOW DAY

Early one morning, Mater awoke to a wonderful surprise. The town of Radiator Springs was completely covered in snow!

"Woo-hoo! Snow day!" he yelled as he threw on his favourite winter hat and drove into town.

Mater was always happy on the first snowfall of the season. But this time it was different. Now his best friend Lightning McQueen was living in Radiator Springs. "I'm going to show Lightning how to *really* have some winter fun!" he exclaimed.

Everyone in town was busy cleaning up the snow. Sheriff and Red had just finished clearing Main Street. The other cars were making sure customers could get into their shops. As Mater pulled into Flo's V8 Café, he saw Lightning. The race car had snow tyres on so he wouldn't slip and slide.

"Hey buddy," said Mater, "looks like you're ready to go play in the snow."

"That's right, Mater," replied Lightning. "Let's hit the slopes!"

Mater and Lightning drove around the corner and saw their friend Ramone. He had just finished giving himself a new paint job. He had white snowflakes on his hood and doors, over an icy shade of blue. Lightning and Mater were impressed!

"Nice paint job, Ramone!" said Lightning. "Can you give me a new look, too?"

"Sure!" the hot rod replied. "I can add some snowflakes that will go great with your shade of red."

Ramone took Lightning and Mater over to his shop and got to work. Soon Lightning was sporting some snowflakes. As soon as Ramone had finished painting, Lightning rushed over to a mirror.

"How do you like your new 'snowstyle'?" asked Ramone.

"It's great!" said Lightning. "Thanks, Ramone!"

"Now it's time to go dashing through the snow!" Mater said. The two friends roared off.

Lightning and Mater rolled through the snow until they reached the top of the largest hill in town.

"Race you to the bottom!" said Mater. "Last one down has a rusty crankshaft!"

"You're on!" replied Lightning. "On your marks, get set... go!"

Lightning was fast, but Mater took the lead. He laughed as he plowed through the snow. Lightning tried to pass him on the right. Mater blocked him. Then Lightning tried to pass him on the left, but Mater swerved in front of him.

"*Snow* way, Lightning!" Mater chuckled. "Try again!"

Halfway down the hill, one of Mater's wheels hit a patch of ice. The tow truck spun around and around until he was driving backwards.

"Watch out below!" he cried as he skidded and crashed into a huge pile of snow.

"You win," said Lightning as he rolled to a stop.

After helping Mater out of the snowbank, Lightning led him over to a frozen lake. Sarge was checking the ice to make sure it wouldn't crack if the cars skated on it.

"It looks okay to me," said Lightning.

"Better safe than sorry," replied Sarge as he moved slowly across the ice. Finally, he called out, "All clear!"

It was time to skate!

Lightning watched Sally glide along the ice. She was a great skater.

*I can do that,* he said to himself as he tried some of her moves.
But he didn't do so well. He slipped and spun around in circles until
he was dizzy.

"You may know a lot about racing," Sally said with a laugh, "but
you still have a few things to learn about ice-skating!" She showed off
her snow tyres, which were helping her stay on track.

Meanwhile, Ramone and Flo were gliding around the ice.

"Slow and low is the way to go, even on the ice and snow," said Ramone.

Luigi and Guido didn't agree. They raced each other across the lake until they were both out of breath. That's when Mater had a great idea for a game. He used his hook and cable to take Luigi and Guido for a spin!

"*Toot-toot*! All aboard the Mater Express!" he yelled as he slowly began to pull his friends faster and faster across the ice.

"We've got speed limits on the ice, too," said Sheriff. "Slow down before someone gets hurt."

"You betcha!" replied Mater, as he pulled Guido and Luigi in a wide loop around Sally and Lightning.

"That looks like fun," said Sally.

"Yeah," said Lightning. "If you can keep your wheels under you." He was still trying to learn to skate.

Everyone was having a wonderful time except for Lizzie. She didn't really like the cold weather.

"This ice is freezing!" she said. "I can't feel the treads on my tyres anymore!"

"Come take a break by the fire," suggested Fillmore. "It's nice and warm over here."

Just as the cars finished skating, the snow began to fall again. Some of the cars started to head back home, but Mater had a better idea.

"Let's catch snowflakes on our tongues!" he said.

Lightning stuck out his tongue like Mater. They drove around trying to catch the falling snow. Before long, Red and Sally joined them!

"This is so much fun!" exclaimed Sally.

Meanwhile, Luigi and Guido were getting ready for a snowball fight. They waited behind a tree with a huge pile. Soon, they saw some of their friends coming down the road.

Guido smiled at Luigi. Then he turned back to the road and launched snowballs at Mater and Lightning.

"Watch out, Mater!" Lightning yelled as he ducked for cover. Mater drove in reverse. He dodged one snowball, then hid behind a tree. But when he peeked out to check if the coast was clear, he saw Guido tossing five snowballs his way.

*"Oww! Ow! Ow! Ow!"* said Mater as the snowballs hit his roof. "Now that's gonna leave a mark!"

A little while later, the cars rolled back into town. The sun was beginning to set. One by one, the neon lights from the storefronts flickered on, lighting up the sky. Everyone stopped to enjoy the beautiful colours that bounced off the clean white snow.

"The town looks great!" said Sally. "It really is a winter wonderland!"

"Sure is!" said Lightning. "Would you like to take a cruise with me down Main Street?" he asked.

"I'd love to!" replied Sally.

Just then, Mater pulled up beside them.

"Did you have a good snow day, Lightning?" asked Mater.

"Honestly," said Lightning, "I didn't have as much fun as I'm going to have tomorrow when I zip past you on that snowy hill!"

"You'd better have a light breakfast," joked Mater, " 'cause you'll be eating lots of snow while you're trying to catch up to me!"

"You're on!" Lightning said with a smile.

After a long day of playing in the snow, all of the cars headed over to Flo's.

"There's nothing better than a warm sip on a cold winter night," said Lightning.

"You're wrong, buddy," replied Mater. "It's better to have friends to share a can with after a long day of fun!"

"You got that right," replied Flo. "Now drink up before it gets cold!"

## The End

# THE STORY
# OF THE FILM

Finn McMissile, a British secret agent, had slipped onto an oil derrick. He was spying on a spectacled criminal named Professor Z.

Finn hid in the rafters and took photos of a TV camera. He also saw another secret agent who had been crushed into scrap metal!

Back in Radiator Springs, race car Lightning McQueen was at the Wheel Well Restaurant. Miles Axlerod – a former oil tycoon – and Italian race car Francesco Bernoulli were on TV. Axlerod was hosting an international race called the World Grand Prix to introduce his new alternative fuel, Allinol. Lightning agreed to join the race.

Lightning and his pit crew soon
arrived in Tokyo for the first race. Mater
embarrassed Lightning at the welcome
party. He even leaked oil beside Axlerod.

Mater raced off to the bathroom. Inside the automated cubicle,
he got poked, prodded and splashed with water!

While Mater was in the cubicle, two members of criminal Professor Z's crew, Grem and Acer, roughed up American Agent Rod "Torque" Redline. When Mater came out of the cubicle, Torque secretly stuck a device underneath Mater.

The following day at the racetrack, Finn
and his fellow agent Holley Shiftwell kept a close
eye on Mater. They thought he was a secret agent, too!

Nearby, Grem and Acer aimed the TV camera at a race car. The
camera was a weapon! Seconds later, the car's engine exploded. Some
thought Allinol was to blame.

Professor Z's gang then went after Mater in the pits. They wanted the device that the American agent had planted on him.

Just as the bad cars were closing in on Mater, Finn rushed in to the rescue. Mater thought he was watching a karate demonstration!

While Mater was distracted, he gave
Lightning bad racing tips. Lightning
ended up losing the race to Francesco! Lightning blamed Mater. "I lost
the race because of you!" he exclaimed.

Mater felt so terrible he decided to go back home. But Finn and Holley whisked him off on a spy mission instead.

Holley removed the planted device from Mater and found a photo of a mysterious, gas-guzzling engine. Mater noticed it had Whitworth bolts, which were very difficult to unscrew.

Meanwhile, Lightning and his team were just outside Porto Corsa, Italy visiting Luigi and Guido's hometown. Lightning talked to Luigi's Uncle Topolino about his fight with Mater.

"Everybody fights now and then, especially best friends," said Uncle Topolino. "But you gotta make up fast."

Holley, Finn and Mater were also on their way to Porto Corsa. Mater had told them the mysterious engine belonged to a Lemon – a car that didn't work right. They soon found out that a secret meeting of Lemons was being held in Porto Corsa. Holley disguised Mater as one of the Lemons' tow trucks so he could sneak into the meeting. She also gave him lots of spy gadgets!

Mater was soon in a room with Professor Z and all the Lemons. Then their "Big Boss", whose identity was hidden, appeared on a TV screen.

He told the Lemons that once Allinol was proven dangerous, all cars would go back to using gasoline. Then the Lemons, who owned most of the world's oil, would become wealthy and powerful.

Outside, the second race had begun. Grem and Acer were on a nearby tower with the camera. They aimed it at the race car from Brazil. Her engine suddenly exploded!

Finn raced to the tower to stop Grem and Acer – but a helicopter captured him with a giant magnet!

Back at the race, Lightning crossed the finish line first! He then announced that he would still be using Allinol in the final World Grand Prix race in London.

The Big Boss heard this and gave the order to get rid of Lightning. Mater used his parachute to escape from the meeting. But before he could warn Lightning, Mater was kidnapped by the Lemons. They had captured Holley, too!

Finn, Holley and Mater were tied up inside the clockworks of Big Bentley in London. Mater finally convinced Finn and Holley that he wasn't a spy.

After the final race began, Grem and Acer told Mater they had planted a bomb inside Lightning's pit. As soon as the Lemons left, Mater escaped, racing to save his best friend.

Minutes later, Holley and Finn escaped, too. They soon discovered the Lemons had actually planted the bomb on Mater! Finn radioed the tow truck to tell him, but Mater was already in the pits.

"Stay away from me!" Mater warned Lightning.

But Lightning still raced forwards to see his best friend!

Meanwhile, Professor Z tried to escape on a combat ship, but Finn stopped him. He tied the Professor up in cables and brought him to Holley, Mater and Lightning.

Then Guido tried to remove the bomb on Mater, but he couldn't unscrew the bolts. Suddenly, everything made sense to Mater. He knew who the Big Boss was!

Mater flew with Lightning to Buckingham Palace. Mater told
everyone that Axlerod was the Big Boss! Mater had figured it out because
the bolts on the bomb were the same Whitworth bolts from the old British
engine in the photo. The engine belonged to Axlerod. He was the biggest
Lemon of all! Axlerod deactivated the bomb and everyone was saved.

Not long after Lightning got back home, he decided to hold his own "Radiator Springs Grand Prix". He invited all the international race cars. Finn and Holley showed up, too. They had come to invite Mater on their next mission. Mater politely turned them down, but he did take his spy gadgets for one last spin! Mater activated his rockets and blasted off down the racetrack, right beside his speedy best friend.

*The End*

# REMATCH!

Lightning McQueen and Francesco Bernoulli had challenged each other to a race in Monza, Italy – Francesco's hometown.

"Benvenuto!" said Francesco. "Your plane was late, but this is no surprise. You will be late crossing the finish line, too."

Lightning smiled. Then he whispered to Mater, "I am so beating him – right here on his own turf!"

As they left the airport, the cars were surrounded by photographers.

"Everyone loves Francesco. He has too many fans," said Francesco.

"Nobody has more fans than Lightning!" Mater piped up.

Francesco rolled his eyes.

"We will prove it!" said Luigi. "Lightning gets hundreds of fan letters each day. Guido, bring the mailbags!" Guido zoomed off!

137

Guido returned with mailbags overflowing with fan letters.

Lightning was a little embarrassed. "Oh, it's really not that big of a deal," he said.

"You are right, Lightning," said Francesco. "It is no big deal because Francesco has much, much more fan mail!"

"Letters are great," said Lightning. "But we like to get some fender-to-fender time with our fans whenever we can."

Lightning and his friends greeted all the cars who were lined up to see them. Mater really got the fans going. They began chanting: "Light-NING! Light-NING!"

"Questo e' ridicolo!" mumbled Francesco. "And what about autographs?" he asked. "Watch – and be amazed."

Francesco started spinning his wheels and spewing out hundreds of autographed photos of himself to his fans. "See? Francesco always gets things done at three hundred kilometres an hour."

After the two racers finished greeting their fans, they drove to a café.

"Hey, Mr Francesco, nobody drinks oil faster than Lightning," said Mater.

"What?" said Lightning. "Mater, I can't drink… "

"C'mon buddy, show 'em what I done taught you!" said Mater. Lightning sighed and managed to finish a can of oil in a few gulps.

Francesco was not impressed. "Francesco never guzzles," he said.

"Oil should be savoured."

Lightning cruised over to Francesco. "How about a warm up before the big race – just you and me?" he asked.

Francesco nodded. "Ah, good idea, Lightning! Try to keep up, if you... "

Before Francesco could finish, Lightning was a red streak down the road! "Ka-ciao, Francesco!" yelled Lightning.

Francesco was just about to catch up with Lightning when he nearly spun out on a left turn.

"How do you make those left turns so well?" Francesco asked Lightning.

"Get equipped with some treaded tyres," said Lightning. "Then turn right to go left. A very good friend taught me that once."

They finally stopped to rest.

Francesco sighed. "Ahh, Italia is beautiful, no? Just like Francesco!"

Lightning chuckled. "Do you always think about yourself?" he asked.

"Of course," said Francesco. "On the racetrack, Francesco only thinks about himself and doing his best. This is why he always wins!"

The next day was the big race. Finally, the world would find out who was the fastest race car! When the flag dropped, the fans went wild! Francesco came out of the first left turn ahead of Lightning. He showed off his new treaded tyres. "Perhaps Lightning has taught Francesco too well!" Lightning couldn't help but smile.

The racers entered the
Monza arena and made a
pit stop.

As Lightning zoomed out
of the pits, he got distracted
by the camera flashes and the
screaming fans.

Suddenly Lightning
remembered what Francesco
had said about focusing on
himself and doing his best.
Lightning looked straight
ahead and took the lead!

As the two cars crossed the finish line, the crowd gasped.

"Ka-chow!" yelled Lightning. "I won!"

"You mean ciao bella," said Francesco. "Francesco won!"

The truth stunned everyone. According to the judges, the race was a... TIE!!!

The cars tried to figure out what to do.

Then Francesco shouted, "No more talk! Talk is slow. What do we do? We race!"

"That's a great idea!" said Lightning. "We'll race in Radiator Springs!"

Then the two fastest cars in the world zoomed away together... to race again another day.

## The End

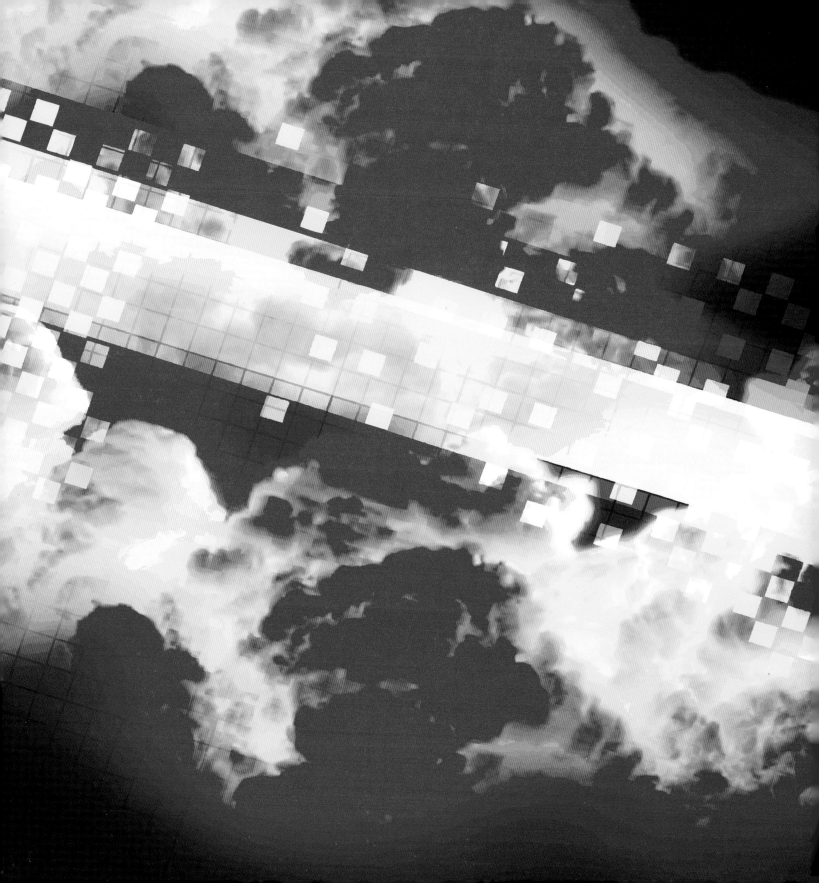